by JANE YOLEN

pictures by BRUCE DEGEN

The Putnam & Grosset Group

 A PaperStar Book, published in 1996 by
The Putnam & Grosset Group, 345 Hudson Street, New York, NY10014.
PaperStar Books and the PaperStar logo are trademarks of
The Putnam Berkley Group, Inc. Originally published in 1985 by
Coward-McCann, Inc., New York. Published simultaneously in Canada.
Manufactured in China
Library of Congress Cataloging-in-Publication Data
Yolen, Jane. Commander toad and the big black hole.
SUMMARY: The space ship Star Warts, commanded by
Commander Toad, encounters a black hole which
threatens the vehicle with doom. [1. Toads—Fiction.
2. Space flight—Fiction. 3. Black hole (Astronomy)—
Fiction]. I. Degen, Bruce, ill. II. Title.
PZ7.Y78Cm 1983 [E] 82-23524
ISBN 978-0-698-11403-6

34 35 36 37 38 39 40

For Sean and Garrett Barry
a couple of toad-al space cadets
—J. Y.

For Renee and Jerry
who lost their marbles
years ago
—B.D.

TOAD ENCOUNTERS:
PLANET OF THE GRAPES
PLANET OF DEEP WADER
PLANET NEPTUNA
WHALEY'S COMET
TAD·POLE STAR
TOADAL ECLIPSE
DIS · ASTEROID
SALAMANDER-LANDE

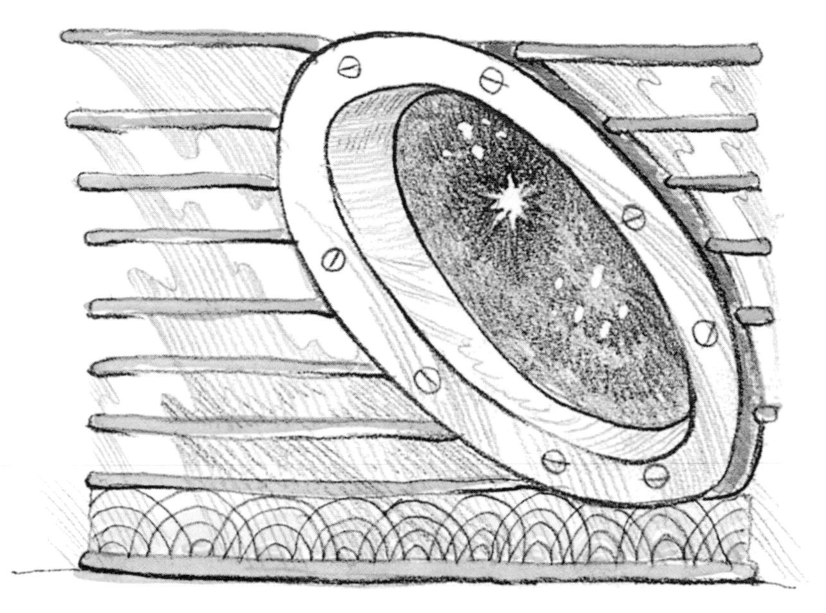

In the star fleet
are many ships.
None is as fast
as the one flown
by Commander Toad.
Brave and bright,
bright and brave,
Commander Toad.

The name of his ship
is *Star Warts*.
Its mission:
to find new worlds,
to explore old galaxies,
to bring a little bit of Earth
out to the alien stars.

Commander Toad
has a tip-top,
hip-hop crew.
Lieutenant Lily
is sharp and quick.
She loves the big machines.

Young Jake Skyjumper
knows the maps and dials.

Mr. Hop
thinks a lot
and knows a lot.
He talks only a little.
And old Doc Peeper
in his grass-green wig
takes good care
of them all.

A trip through space
means many meals.
Hot meals
and cold meals.
Good meals
and bad meals.
Sweet meals
and salty meals
and meals just in between.

But on a spaceship
all the meals
look the same.
"They look like pills,"
grumps old Doc Peeper.

"They look like bullets,"
grumbles Lieutenant Lily.
"They look like marbles,"
sighs Jake.
"They look like eyes
looking up at me,"
says Mr. Hop.

Commander Toad smiles.
“My mother always said,
Don’t talk
with your mouth full,”
he warns.
The little round
food pellets
pop out of his mouth
and spatter all over.

"See what happens?"
Lieutenant Lily shakes her head.
"You must have had
a very messy toad hole."

Old Doc Peeper
looks out the window.
"I do not know
if the hole ahead of us
is good,
or if it is clean,
but it is certainly
BLACK."

“A black hole!”
says the crew.
Mr. Hop thinks
long and hard and deep.
“No one knows
what lives
in a black hole.”

Jake's voice goes all quivery.
"Something *lives*
in that big black hole?"
he asks.
"Of course,"
says Mr. Hop,
looking up from the table.
"On Earth
all kinds of animals
live in holes."

"Toads live in holes,"
says Commander Toad.
Mr. Hop ignores him.
"Out here in space
it is the same.
A hole is a house
for someone."
"Or something,"
says young Jake,
doing a good job
of scaring himself.

Commander Toad smiles.
"On Earth
my mother and I
had a very nice hole.
It had seven rooms
and a back porch
overlooking a lake.
I sat and sang there
on summer nights."
Old Doc Peeper
clears his throat.
"Toads cannot sing.
Only frogs can sing."

Commander Toad
clears *his* throat.
"Of course toads can sing.
And *Commander* Toads
sing best of all."
He sings:
"Oh give me a hole
By the side of a mole,
Where the deermice
And jackrabbits play. . . ."

His mouth is open
but his eyes are closed
He does not see
that no one else
likes his singing.

Lieutenant Lily
holds her
star fleet nosekerchief
to her head.
"Doc is right,"
she says.
"Toads cannot sing.
Toads croak out of tune
and growly.
Especially Commander Toads.
Only frogs can sing."
"Toads!" says Commander Toad.
"Frogs!" says the crew.

And there is an argument
that is almost
a mutiny,
except just then there is a
BUMP
and a mighty
THUMP
and the *Star Warts* stops moving.

"We are stuck in space,"
calls out Jake.
Commander Toad
peers out a porthole.
"We are not stuck *in* space,
we are stuck *on* something."

The others look out.
Sure enough,
Commander Toad is right.
The ship is stuck
on something.
Something long.
Something pink.
Something very sticky.

“What do you suppose that
something
long and pink and sticky is?”
asks Lieutenant Lily.
“Space bubble gum?”

"I haven't got
the froggiest notion,"
says Commander Toad.
"In all my years
in star fleet
I have never seen anything
quite like it."

Mr. Hop
shakes his head.
He has fed the facts
about the long and pink
and very sticky something
into the computer.
The computer looks sick.
It does not have
the froggiest notion either.

Old Doc Peeper
scratches under his wig
with a stick.
"I see those every day,"
he says.
"That long and pink
and very sticky something
is a tongue.
A giant tongue."
"A tongue!"
says the crew.

Just then
the tongue starts moving
toward the black hole.
The starship
moves with it.
Closer
and closer
and closer still.

Suddenly they hear a noise.
It sounds like a song.
The song goes like this:
Look out teeth,
Here comes tongue,
Over the gullet
And here I come!

The ship shakes all over.
"I do not like
the sound of that song,"
says Mr. Hop.
"It is out of tune,"
says Lieutenant Lily.
"And growly."

"I don't like the sound
of that song either,"
says Commander Toad,
"because what
it sounds like is . . ."
"LUNCH!"
screams young Jake Skyjumper.

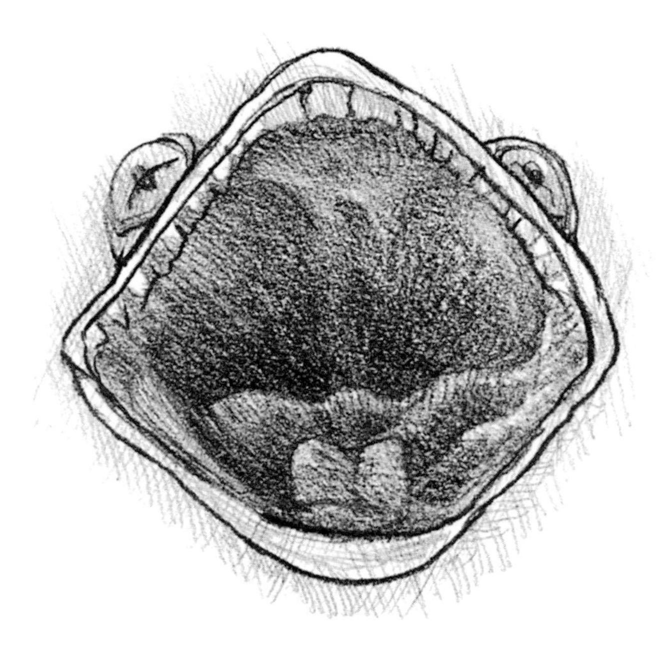

"That is not a big black hole,
that is a big black mouth!
And it belongs to
an E.T.T!"
An E.T.T.
They all shudder.
An E.T.T.
is an
Extra Terrestrial Toad.

Jake presses
thirteen buttons
and turns seven wheels,
but the *Star Warts*
is still stuck
and still moving.

Lieutenant Lily
shoves the engines
into reverse.
The tongue shudders
for a minute,
then moves again.
The black hole gets nearer.
And bigger.
And wider.
"Quick,"
says Commander Toad.
"Everyone into the sky skimmer."

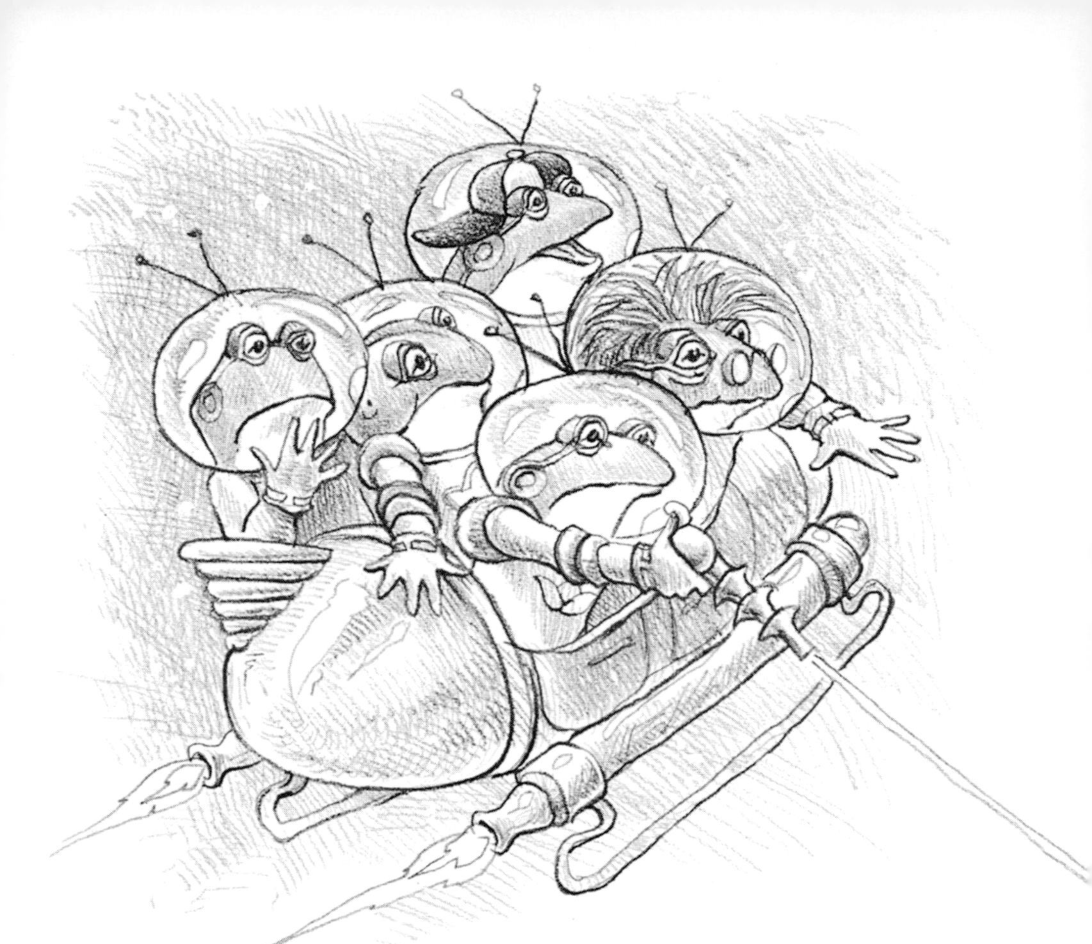

They put on
their space suits
and helmets
and scramble
into the skimmer.
The skimmer hovers
above the tongue.

Lieutenant Lily
aims her gun
and shoots.
One . . . two . . . three.
She never misses,
but she only raises
blisters like bubbles
on the giant tongue.
"Now what?"
asks Mr. Hop.
"I have an idea,"
says old Doc Peeper.

He points.
Jake guides the skimmer
into the hole.
It is very dark
and toothy
inside the hole.
Doc leans over the side
of the skimmer
with a long pole
and pokes it at the tongue.

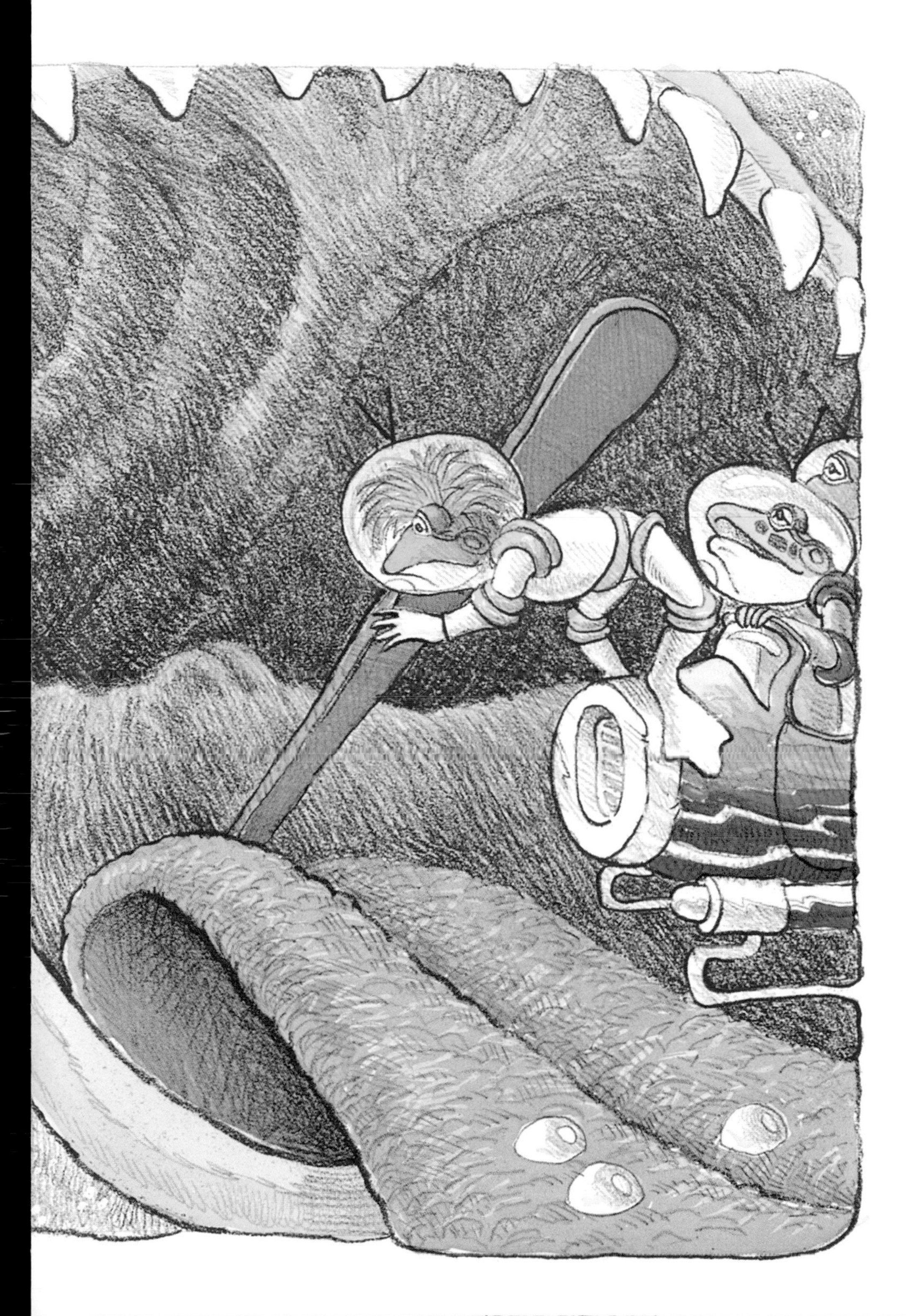

Jake puts the skimmer
into reverse.
It goes backward.
But the *Star Warts*
goes forward
toward the hole,
the big black hole.

“Now what?”
asks Mr. Hop.
“Only one thing left,”
says Commander Toad.
“My secret weapon.”
“Secret weapon?”
says Lieutenant Lily.
“Nothing is stronger
than my gun.”

Commander Toad smiles.
"This is toad-al
all-out war,"
he says.
"Listen—and learn."
He turns up
his microphone.
His voice
booms out into the dark.

"Oh give me a hole . . ."
he sings.
The others hold their ears.
"By the side of a mole . . ."
The microphone makes
his voice loud.
It does not make
his voice good.
"Where the deermice . . ."

Suddenly there is
another loud and growly voice
singing along
with Commander Toad.

"AND JACKRABBITS
PLAY. . . ."
As the voice sings,
its tongue moves
up and down
up and down
up and down again.
It jars the spaceship left
and right
and back
and forth.

On the last note
the tongue flings
the *Star Warts*
into space.
"Follow that ship,"
says Commander Toad.

The skimmer zooms
and catches up
to the *Star Warts*
just left of the Milky Way.
They board the ship,
tired and happy.

“How did you know
what to do?”
asks Mr. Hop,
as they sit down
around the table.

“Yes, Commander,”
says Lieutenant Lily.
“When my gun
and Doc’s
tongue depressor
did not work,
how did you know
what to do?”

"I remembered back
to my tadpole days,"
says Commander Toad,
"when my mother
used to say,
Don't sing . . ."
Doc Peeper grinned.
"She knew you well."

“My mother used to say,
Don’t sing
with your mouth full . . .”
The crew laughs.
“*Don’t sing*
with your mouth full
lest your food
fall off your tongue.”

Mr. Hop nods his head.
“Your mother
was very wise,” he says.
“And so,” says Doc Peeper,
“is her son.”
They all eat a hearty meal
that looks like
pills or bullets
or marbles or eyes,
but no one complains,
and no one sings
until they are done.

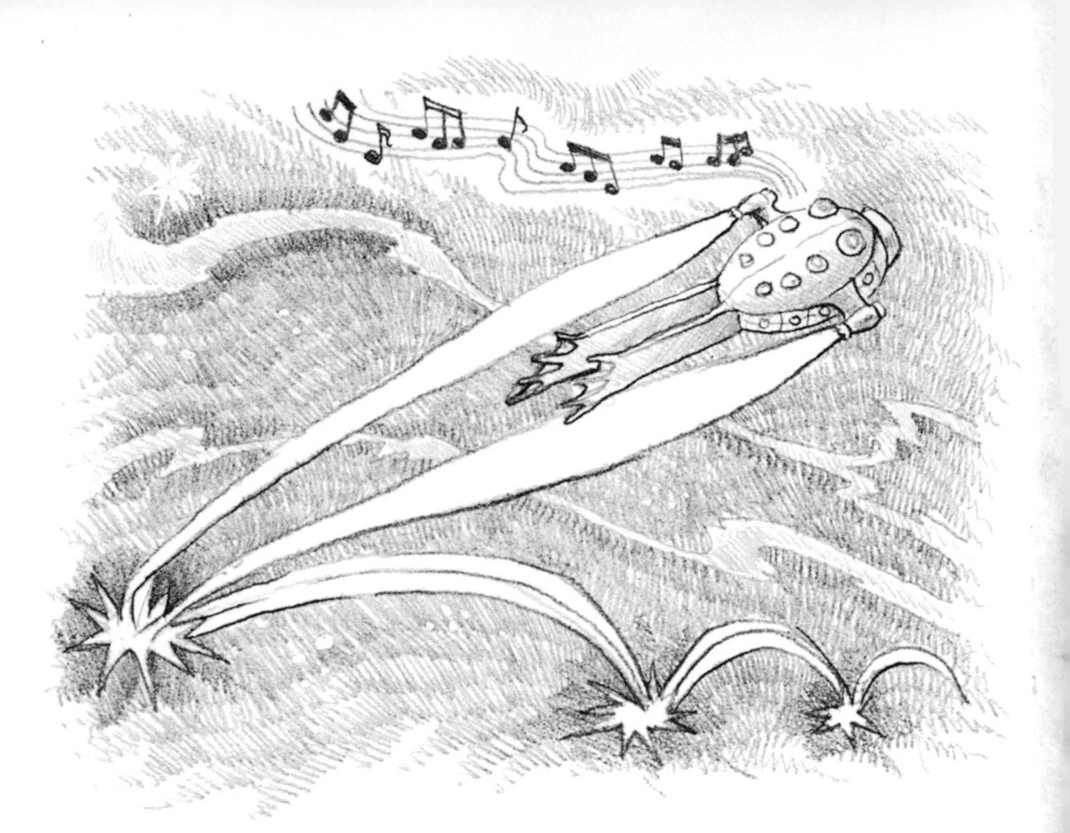

Then,
with a loud chorus
of "Oh Give Me A Hole"
ringing through the ship,
the *Star Warts*
leapfrogs
across the galaxy
from star
to star
to star.